For two places I love,

Mexico and L.A.,

and for the people there

☆

TONY JOHNSTON

Any Small Goodness

a novel of the barrio

ILLUSTRATIONS BY
RAÚL COLÓN

SCHOLASTIC INC.
New York Toronto London Auckland Sydney
Mexico City New Delhi Hong Kong Buenos Aires

With appreciation to those who read the manuscript
and gave me their insights: Denia Camacho, Al Mantini,
Rydell Pulido, "Bear" Sanchez, Salvador Villar,
and my family, who helped *excesivamente*.

My deep thanks to Bonnie Verburg.
Without her, there would be no book.

Poem epigraphs that appear in this book
without credit were written by the author.

Designed by Kathleen Westray.

*L*os Angeles is a place of movie stars
and fast cars and people who are too rich
and people who are too poor.
An area of freeway chases and drive-bys
and death. That's what some people
will quickly point out.

☆

But there's another L.A., where warmth
and humor and humanity pervade.
Where a *taquería* sign declares:
ONE CAUSE, ONE PEOPLE, ONE TACO.

☆

This is an L.A. as real as there is.
Good things happen here.

For everyone who gives up

a part of himself

✫

American Names

I have fallen in love with American names,

the sharp names that never get fat . . .

— from "American Names,"
Stephen Vincent Benét

My name's Arturo, "Turo" for short. For my father, and my grandfather, and *his* father, back and back. Arturos — like stacks of strong adobe bricks, forever, my grandmother says.

Really, my name *was* Arturo. Here's why: Three years ago our family came up from Mexico to L.A. From stories they'd heard, my parents were worried for our safety in "that hard-as-a-fist Los Angeles." But Papi needed better work.

Rosa, my little sister, wailed, "'Nighted States, no! Too dark!" My brother, Luis, and I pretty much clammed up. I guess numbed by the thought of leaving our home, and a little scared, too, about the tough barrio.

Like some random, windblown weeds, we landed in L.A., home to movie stars and crazies and crazy movie stars.

Luckily, I had some English when I got here. "It is good to have Eeenglish in your pocket," my parents pressed us always, *"por las cochinas dudas."* For the dirty doubts, that is. Just in case. So, for the dirty doubts, we've all got a little English.

☆

In school, I get Miss Pringle. Miss Pringle's

okay, I guess, but if scientists studied her brain, I bet they'd find it to be a large percentage of air. She's always kind of floating where she goes, and talking in a bright and airy way. My friend Raúl says she's got "excessive sparkle." Raúl loves weird words.

ANYWAY, first day of school, Miss Pringle, all chipper and bearing a rubbery-dolphin smile, says, "Class, this is Arthur Rodriguez." Probably to make things easier on herself. Without asking. *Ya estuvo.* Like a used-up word on the chalkboard, Arturo's erased.

Who cares? Not me. With such a name as Arthur, I'll fit in at this school real well. Like a pair of chewed-up Nikes. Not stiff and stumblingly new. American names are cool. Frank. Mike. Jake. They sound sharp as nails shot from guns.

I'm not the only one who's been gringo-ized. There's Jaime and Alicia and Raúl. Presto change-o! With one breath of teacher-magic, they're James and Alice and Ralph. (Our friend Lloyd, alias Rat Nose, is already a gringo, so his name's untouchable.)

When we're together, we joke about our new names.

"So, 'mano," Raúl says with bravura (another one of his words), "how's it feel to be Arthur, like a Round Table guy?"

"*Muy* cool." I slip into full *pocho*, an English-Spanish mix. "Hey, Alice," I say.

"Yeah?"

"Seen Alicia?"

She scans the hall. Digs in her backpack. "No, man. She's *gone*."

We all laugh. But I notice Alicia's eyes, like two dark and hurting bruises. I fluff it off, easy as dandruff flakes in a TV ad.

My parents hate that I'm Arthur. I mean, totally H-A-T-E. I can tell because when I break this news, my mother starts cooking excessively.

Her way of organizing the world. My father goes carefully quiet.

Most parents I know would spit out choice curses if their children chose names that hurt their ears. Maybe even smack them. Not mine. Mami and Papi are like two soft doves. They work on a policy of gentleness. They've never touched us in anger. Never talked severely. So their silent disfavor hits harder than the sting of slaps.

Tough tortillas. I'm going gringo.

Who hates my name most is my *abuelita*. Grandmother always dresses in cricket-black, in *luto* for my grandfather, who died. She's eighty-something. So old, her skin looks like it's woven from brown cobwebs. She's got two braids wound so high on her head, they must have been growing during her whole life. Unlike my parents, Abuelita's no dove. Like a little fighting rooster, she's got bravura to spare.

Even though she's feisty, God guides her life.

She closes most conversation with an after-breath of *"Dios mediante,"* God willing.

Since Grandfather died, she lives with us. She came all the way from Aguascalientes, Mexico, on a Norteño bus, with only her prayer book, a photograph of Grandfather, and her *molcajete.*

A *molcajete*'s a three-legged grinding stone, carved of lava spit from some old volcano. It's hollowed and pitted, like a cupped hand scarred with acne. Abuelita uses it to grind chilies. For salsa and stuff. Takes longer than forever. Jeez! She could do it with one *zzzzzip* of the blender switch! If that lava-lump was mine, I'd chuck it out.

"Theeesss name Arter — eeet burns in my earsss like poissson." Since my Spanish's a little crippled from pouring the English on, Abuelita hisses her English to be sure I can't escape her point. *Muele, muele, muele.* She grinds her disfavor into me at every chance.

The heat of peppers fills her voice as she pulverizes chilies extra vigorously, for some tasty Mexican dish. If my new name were a chili pepper, she'd pulverize that, too.

At every chance she turns "Arturo" on her tongue, like a pearl.

What does *she* know, this thin-as-an-eyelash old woman from Hot Waters, Mexico? Man, this is L.A. To get by, you need American names.

Apart from problems of names, here there are problems of gangs. Like those saber-toothed tigers in pits of tar, kids get sucked into them. For protection from invaders from other areas. Or to have a place to go, or something to do. Even some old guys, fathers with kids, are gang members.

My father's the kind of person who removes his hat in a restaurant and blesses his plate of tacos. Not prime gang material. I hope I'm not, either. Though the pull at school is pretty strong, I keep looking for something else to do.

My friends live on my block. All the time they come over to hang out in Abuelita's kitchen. They're there now, dragged by their noses. By the pure power of chili dust. And the tang of cilantro.

When they enter, she pinches their cheeks and claims they are *"muchachos muy lindos"* and calls them by their true names: Jaime, Alicia, Raúl.

"Hola, Lloyd." She aims a dripping spoon straight for Rat Nose. "You love *menudo?* You taste."

Abuelita speaks with such excessive bravura, each name scrapes my mind like the *scritch-scritching* claws of a feisty rooster.

"Jeez!" I say to myself, cringing with shame. But my friends seem totally unfazed. Even pleased. Raúl's got a heart tattoo (not real, just inked on). It's so big, it blues his muscle. Grinning, he pumps his tattoo for Abuelita. *¡Caray!* Don't they remember? We peeled off those old names, like onion skins. Still, a worm of doubt squirms in my mind.

My friends slump themselves over the arms of chairs like overcooked noodles and chat easily with my grandmother. Alice's eyes — at the sound of her real name, they flame up, bright with excessive sparkle. *Por* please!

☆

Around this time we have our first run-in with the police. Really, Mami does.

In our yard we've got trees, so we've got *tlacuaches,* possums. Mami's a calm one, except when it comes to these. Personally, I like them with their glass-bead eyes and little pink snouts. But like some people've got dread of snakes, Mami's got possum-*pavor.* She's convinced they'll give her *tlacuachazos,* big possum hits, when she takes the garbage out at night.

Once when Papi's on a sales trip, she has this crisis. At 4 A.M., something's rattling outside. A garbage can. From her experience with garbage and L.A. wildlife, Mami immediately knows what this is. She can't sleep from the sounds, but she can't touch a can full of possums, either. So she calls 911.

"*¡Tlacuaches! ¡Tlacuaches!*" she screams into the phone.

"Apaches, ma'am?"

"*¡TLACUACHES!*" As if louder will make this come clear.

Someone must ask what she's talking about, because she says, "Send someone now — who speaks *Eeenglish*!"

We're all waiting when five police come. Armed for a world war. They dump the poor, dazed-out possum from the garbage drum and severely tell Mami about using the 911 code, set up for emergencies only. Then they leave.

Mami's still convinced of the wrong of this. For her, it's a textbook case of 911. To this day she huffs, "What do polices know, in their blue uniforms?"

☆

One night I'm struggling with geography homework. Trying to map out where Marco Polo went. *Hijos,* did that guy get around! His route looks like some bad knitter's tangled yarn. Like my sister Rosa's when she's trying to learn.

Through the blinds, my room's banded with moon. Everything's quiet. Even the crickets are sleeping. Then I hear something. Mumbling. Coming from Abuelita's room. Our rooms are back to back. Like when you check your size against somebody else.

My room's painted white. But Abue's, it's totally Mexican pink, the color she believes the Mexican flag should be. Her walls dance with *calacas,* skeletons, of all sizes and materials — clay, wood, wire, papier-mâché. Abue thumbs her nose at Death.

Abuelita's talking to Grandfather, muttering to the ghost of his photograph, I bet.

"Arturo," she says, holding that word in her mouth gently, like a highly breakable egg. She speaks Spanish only.

"He's a good boy, our Turo. Just a little bit

mixed up. One day, *Dios mediante,* he will recognize how good is your name. One day he will know what it means — Arturo. He is me. He is you. And all before. And all to come."

I hear a long, moist sigh then. Like the breath of a tired teakettle. I hear tears glaze her voice. I feel a blaze of embarrassment to be listening in on this private conversation.

My heart feels squeezed out. Abuelita has known all along what I should have known. It's okay to be Arturo. What a *menso*-head I am. *Un idiota de primera.* To give up my name. It's to give up my family. To let myself — all of us — be erased to chalkboard dust.

In this moment my history holds me. Like a warm *sarape.* I feel tears come. In this moment I want to hug Abuelita.

I look out my window. At the half-moon. Like a perfectly broken button.

It's late. But I call my friends anyhow.

"*Por* please," I joke, "come over."

"*¿Ahora?*"

"Now. *Ahoritita.*"

And they come — Ralph and Alice and James and Rat Nose — all expectant and wondering what in *diablos* is going on. Before any of them can wedge a word in, I blurt, "We're taking back our names. We don't, we're *borrados.* Blotted out."

"You mean 'Rat Nose' is dead?" Ralph moans. "Such an *excelente* and rodential name?"

"Rat Nose lives. We'll call ourselves whatever we want, but those teachers can't make us into someone new. Those teachers, they must be *formal.*"

They're pretty cool with that. Especially Alice. Little stars bloom in her eyes. Ralph's already itching for morning, he says, so he can apprise Miss Pringle. I itch to apprise my family, now snoring deeper than zombies. Especially Abuelita.

We make a pact. Right there in her chili-laden kitchen. On the most Mexican thing around —

one by one we place our hands on Abuelita's *mol-cajete,* ugly as a pockmarked thug.

In solemn ceremony we retrieve our names. Our selves. Into the bold night air we say with utmost bravura:

¡Raúl!

¡Alicia!

¡Jaime!

¡Lloyd!

¡Arturo!

When we apprise her of our stand on names, Miss Pringle's pretty surprised. But she limps along with it. (A result of "the incident" is that other kids go for their own "name-reclaimment.")

☆

Not long after, they're selling T-shirts and plants and stuff at school. To raise funds for a computer. I buy a little cactus, prickly to touch and with one red bloom.

After school, I give it to Abuelita: "Ta-*ta*!" She

laughs when I spring it from behind my back, and she hugs me with the gift between us, but somehow we don't get poked.

"*¡Ay, Arturo, mi pequeño cactus!*" Abuelita exclaims. Like I'm prickly sometimes, but have a chance of flowers.

Abuelita's prickly but full of goodness. As far from gangbangers as Papi is. I wish I could be like her, getting people's names back for them — or something important like that. So far I'm just hanging out. Being like some weird L.A. weather report: prickly — with a chance of flowers.

Corn Fungus

There's a hero on the corner,
going in disguise —
tennis shoes and Ray-Bans,
ragged old Levi's.

— poem

*O*ur cat's called Huitlacoche. For the black-as-night fungus of corn which our family loves to eat, squished and spiced with onion and garlic and chilies. Cooked up, it looks pretty much like swamp glug. But its taste is like some food of heaven.

Behind our house, Abuelita's got a corn plot which she cares for with tenderness. Day and night a small scarecrow shuffles over it, draped with a tattered *rebozo*. Each year, when the plants show first green, Abuelita's out there, too, chanting them up. With small prayers for height and flavor. Small prayers mostly for *huitlacoche*.

"Diosito," she says in her cobwebby voice, "bless this corn with large quantities of fungus." For best results, she repeats the request in Náhuatl, an ancient tongue I don't understand. Abuelita's willing to call upon all gods for help. Not just Jesús alone. Some people might bristle about this tactic. I say it's smart to cover your bases.

The fungus affects the kernels themselves. If all goes well, in our family opinion, the yellow nubs will blight and swell to the size of grapes; to the color and softness of baby mice.

ANYWAY, about our cat. She's pretty goofy-looking. From a run-in with a door, her face is a little flat, and her tongue-tip sticks out always, like a soft pink dart. She seems pleased to be called for corn fungus, becoming one big purr at the sound of her name.

Under the table, at mealtimes, Huitla gives us soft nudges, hopeful for snacks. Or she sleeps on us in a warm curl while we watch TV. We totally adore her.

Sometimes she brings just the rubbery tail of a rat she's murdered into the house. Because she adores us back — and because she ate the rest. Huitla's a definite part of our family — until Mega Mango, my brother's band, is born.

Luis's in high school, but still too young to drive. That's the low thing in his life.

Rhythms rush through his blood with such force, side by side with him I seem half asleep. Flairless, while he puts flair on everything. He's always snapping his fingers to some inside beat, swaying his body like a dazed snake.

Abuelita explains the reason: His *nahual,* like a birth animal, is Ozomatli, the Aztec monkey god of music. So it's not surprising he taught himself to play an instrument. The trumpet's his torture-mode of choice, Papi says, in a way that shows he's proud.

Once dominating the trumpet, it's only a matter of time till Luis forms a band. I think it's cool he does this, but I don't say so, or he'd swell like a blowfish, with *orgullo.* Flairless me. No chance of pride-filled swell-ups.

ANYWAY, I don't exactly ooze musical promise, and I'm a little kid to Luis. Still, from pity, probably, he lets me play the gourd in the band. The gourd works by rasping its ribbed edge with a stick till it shrieks, *Crrrrrink!* Pretty lame, as instruments go. I don't care. I'd play a *cucaracha* to be in Mega Mango.

The band practices in our garage, nearly throbbing the whole place down. Right away, we make a pact with the neighbors, limiting "musical" hours. "Musical" is in quotes, since some neighbors consider our sound totally noise. Most love it, really, I think. Sometimes I see them stop pulling weeds or scattering fertilizer, and break into their own private dance steps.

☆

One day, Huitla makes the big mistake of napping in the garage. No one notices the cat. But when we blast forth, she sure notices *us*. Takes off like swarms of demon dogs are raking her heels with razor-teeth! Man! Talk about flying fur!

I forget all about her wild escape. Till night.

Mami's stirring the various pots that will become dinner. "Where's Huitla?" she asks. Because that cat has always twined around her legs when food's available, nearly tripping her sometimes. Mami doesn't mind. She always stops cooking, stoops her dove-shaped body down, giving Huitla a little pat. "*Ay,* Huitla, old black lump," she croons gently. "One day you will simply break Mami's old neck. Then what will those greedy ones do for a cook?" She chuckles a lot, she finds herself so humorous.

"That Huitla," Mami repeats. "*¿Dónde está?*"

Luis gouges a taste of refried beans from a saucepan. "*No sé.*" He grunts.

"She took off," I say, in explanation of everything.

Things are pretty quiet at dinner. Except for cat questions. We're all wondering where Huitla's gone. Rosa wanders from room to room. "Huitla!" She calls over and over. "*Ven,* kitty! Come!"

But she doesn't. Not tonight. Not any night.

From the start we search everywhere. All of Huitla's favorite spots. Like beside the scarecrow in the corn plot, where she loves to plop her lazy self down, in the fullest sun. The neighbors help. They love our little cat for her sweetness. And for her funky stuck-out tongue.

With Crayolas, Rosa makes a sign. Just the face of a little black cat, poking out the tip of its tongue. MY KITTY IS LOST, she writes, with our help, and gives the number of our telephone.

☆

It's two weeks since we've seen her. Now a little silence moves through the house, as if filling Huitla's space. Nobody ever says so, but maybe we guess she's dead. Or at least that she won't return.

Abuelita has her words of comfort to say. "We will find her, *Dios mediante*."

Rosa's the one most desolate. She sometimes crawls into my lap and says nothing, just sucks her thumb.

☆

It's a typical night at home. Rosa's blabbling into a big plastic bottle, squeaking like Alvin the Chipmunk. Luis's blazing out *"Chango"* on the radio.

"Turn it down, I'm trying to study!" I shout.

"Well, try harder!"

Above the blare, the phone rings.

"*¡Zafo!*" Luis yells, which means "dibs not answering."

"*¡Zafo!*" Rosa echoes.

Though she's sitting close, Abuelita also refuses to answer. *Or speak face-to-face, or don't speak at all,* is her thought on the subject of telephones. Given the chance, she'd throw it off a cliff.

I dash up and take the call. At first, there's only breathing on the line.

"Hello?"

At last a voice comes. "Hello. This is Leo Love speaking."

This is Leo Love breathing, I think.

Leo Love! *¡Caray!* It's got to be one of those crank romantic calls you hear about sometimes! I don't want to become involved in anything weird, so I nearly hang up.

"I've got Hoo — Hoo —" The voice makes frustrated-owl calls, then just blurts, "I've got your cat."

"Huitlacoche!" I shout into the receiver.

"Yes, Hootlecooch," the man agrees.

Over a series of explosions of joy in the room,

I take the guy's *datos* down. Name, address, tele-phone. I say, "We're on our way."

And we are, all of us piling into Papi's car, Valentín. Laughing, all ecstatic. And crying.

Valentín goes jittering down the streets, slowing, speeding up, sometimes stopping in full so we can check the directions. We're all so anxious. When we reach the given address, it seems like we've been driving forever. Actually, it's not many blocks.

Mr. Leo Love doesn't need to hear his doorbell. We arrive in such an excitement, he can't miss us. He opens the door.

He's an old white guy, wire-bearded and small. No Mr. Universe, but more with the build of a sparrow. Pants creased sharp enough to slice *chorizo*. Dressed in tweed, so he looks like he's wrapped in tree bark. He talks stiff as bark, too. Like every word makes a difference to his life.

Then, suddenly, he nearly blasts his bark off with a sneeze. A chorus of *salud*s follows.

Quickly, Abuelita holds out a lime from her lumpy purse. She never travels without limes.

Leo Love looks surprised.

"You take this," she orders him. "Good for all things."

He lamely takes the lime.

"I am allergic to cats," he says, embarrassed, holding out Huitla.

"*Limones* good also for that," says Abuelita.

By now, Rosa's popcorning up and down so much that for safety, Leo Love hands the cat to Mami.

Squashed-in face. Tip of pink tongue flagging out. It's our cat, all right.

"Hey, Fish Breath," Luis greets her. Words of love, for him.

What's the next step? Everyone's in confusion. Everyone except Abuelita. She bustles up and embraces this stranger. Plants kisses on his tortilla-white cheeks.

"*Estimado* Señor Mister Leo Love," she says with fervor, "you are a most very good hero."

Señor Mister Leo Love seems amazed by that. And touched. In confusion, he invites us into his immaculate house. Everyone sits in a perched position, the furnishings are so clean. Mami's eyes survey the room. They say that she loves his housekeeping.

Leo Love offers coffee. We all accept. In her excitement, even Rosa. This is a happy time. I guess that's why Mami allows it. Anyway, when Rosa's done, it's not coffee. Just some pale gunk, mainly sugar, so thick it could hold bricks together.

While Rosa glugs this down, she never lets go of Huitla. (Now that she's semi-settled down, Mami allows Rosa to hold the cat.)

On her chair, Abuelita leans forward. Like a small and eager bird. We await the prize words that are surely coming.

"Now, Señor Mister Leo Love," she says with respect and careful words, like taking careful steps on stairs, "how arrived our sweet little *gatita* to your door?"

Somehow Leo Love has followed this thick braid of conversation. He sips his coffee and says, "Actually, she did not arrive at the door. I discovered her near my avocado tree."

"I do not wish to seem rude," says Papi, who has never seemed rude in his whole life. "But two weeks —"

Leo Love nods his head. "Yes. It is certainly a long time not to communicate. However, there was nothing to identify her."

Huitla has tags. From the vet. He even had to make them two times, because of problems of spelling.

"She had no tags," he continues. "And I have allergies. But, what could I do? I decided that at my age, I had earned the right to throw caution away. I decided to keep the little creature. I hadn't much else to offer, so I fed her trout."

A shadow skims Mami's face. It seems to mean, *I cannot compete with trout.* Leo Love goes on.

"However, all the trout in the world could not

assuage my guilt. Someone must miss her terribly. A child, most probably. Today, I searched the rescue site again, and by good fortune found the cat's collar. Broken. It was precisely then that I dialed your number."

At that, Abuelita perks up. She puts two and two together fast. "You believe in God?" She bores into him, all energized.

Leo Love looks at her as if seeing a blink of new light about this situation. He says, "It is something always worth considering."

For the moment, that satisfies Abuelita.

Then, like a meteor shooting on a wild course, Rosa asks, "Will you be my pen pal?"

Even though he lives so close she could spit about as far as his house, he agrees.

When we leave, Leo Love asks, "Hootlecooch, what sort of name is that?"

Abuelita explains, "It's Mexico — for corn fungus."

Leo Love looks stunned.

"Soon I bring you some."

And she will. And she'll see that he eats it, too.

☆

We've thanked Leo Love so much, he's retreated. We're outside the house, standing under the avocado tree. A slight breeze breathes by. The rustle of leaves sounds like I'm inside a flight of birds.

The newspaper boy wheels up in a gravelly crunch.

"That your cat?" he asks, eyeing Huitla.

"Yeah."

"What a pain!"

We all ask what he means.

"Mr. Love spent a whole night in that tree," he says, pointing to where we are. "Baby-sitting the cat. He's kinda old. And a handful of cat — plus fear of falling — kept him up there."

"How do you know this?" Papi asks.

"I found him. Next morning. Firemen got 'em down."

☆

The day flames out in a smog-sunset, a wild gift of L.A.

On the way home Papi says, "This Leo Love is a brave man. In spite of fear he saved Huitla. When no eyes are upon him, that is a person's true test."

I file this inside of myself. Maybe one day when no eyes are on me, I'll have a true test, too.

☆

Now Huitla's home. Sleeping on the sofa in a happy sprawl of fur. I sit beside her, totally sunken down. Our sofa's so soft, sitting on it's like being swallowed by a clam. I think about old Leo Love, who Abue now calls *El Estimado*, The Esteemed One. Going against allergies and dizziness and possible broken bones to save our cat.

You could do worse than be like such a person.

The Coach

If you find yourself on the Mountain,
either you've always lived here,
or you've wandered badly....
— *L.A. Times*, February 2, 1999

My hair wakes up stupid. Finally I tame it with some product like axle grease, throw down *chilaquiles*, and head for school, dreading first period, basketball, when I'm grogged with sleep.

Another day in L.A., a long time after our name-reclaimment. Three years, to be exact. With Alicia and Raúl and Jaime, I walk through the morning built from haze. Late summer heat's still got a choke hold on the city, so, although it's early, everywhere you look you see things in semi-wilt. People, trees, lawns. Even the streets stretch out like parched grey tongues.

I feel listless as a sunstroked lettuce. Probably my friends do, too. To avoid any excess outlay of energy, we don't talk much. Don't even kick the beer cans that crud up the sidewalk.

Suddenly, these older guys ram us from behind, elbows swinging like steel chicken wings. Tattooed-up *mensos* in leather jackets, emblemized with Death.

They snarl, *"¡Muévete, buey!"* And they don't mean a barnyard animal.

They swagger us out of their way, so close I'm nearly blown down by beer breath. At 8 A.M.!

Who's the buey? I think. I want to break and run but know better. Never show fear. *Stay cool,* I tell myself. *Just walk.* With *cholos* like these, you can be assured there are *cuetes*, guns, somewhere here.

When they're past, they laugh and flip us off and, luckily, keep careening down the street. We're mute the rest of the way.

☆

My day's started sour. First my hair, then punks, now what?

Man, what a *menso*-head I am, signing up for sports. And at this torturous hour.

Why did I go for this crack-of-dawn pain? Inside myself where hope sits, I guess I thought maybe I'd flower immediately into a basketball star. So far this hasn't happened. Not immediately or otherwise. I'm not exactly *Señor Coordinación.* My ability's sub-*excelente,* but I don't trip myself, either.

Ours is a barrio of basketball maniacs. Our fans don't wear cheese hunks on their heads like some of those *idiotas* on TV. But they get pretty into the game. When the season approaches, like now, too-worn shoes stop and start, with no squeak. Too-soft balls loft through the air. The whole neighborhood starts dribbling and jumping around. Like a great big popcorn machine. Guess that's another reason I signed up. Like the ad says, "I love this game!"

☆

Now we're in the gym, waiting for Coach. He comes late a lot because he owns a Timex as primitive as a sundial and a car that's easily Jurassic.

"I count on every one of you players," Coach pounds into us again and again. "I can't count on my watch; I can't count on my car; I've *got* to count on something."

Everyone's about as hazed-out as me. So there's a spurt of talk now and then, but mostly pretty senseless mumblings. Some kids stretch out on the bleachers for extra z's.

Our school colors are orange and green. Our mascot's the tiger. What *menso*-heads thought these things up? Tigers don't exist in that color combination. Tigers don't exist in L.A.

ANYWAY, dressed like peas and carrots, our basketball class's waiting for Coach, *again*.

Unbelievable! Coach strolls into the gym — in a suit! With a tie! (Off to one side, like a skinny, wind-flopped flag.) He usually wears grey over-sized sweats that make him look like a melting elephant. Today he's dressed sharp.

The reason's standing beside him. Seven-foot plus, with the build of a post, and bald as a light-bulb. An NBA basketball player once so famous he made Santa Claus seem like a total unknown. He's been out of the game a while, but any true fan knows him. *¡Caray!* The day's shaping up!

What I notice most about this guy is his eyes. Like owls'. It seems there are deep things in them. Deep and mysterious.

What's he doing lost among the Tigers? He must have really veered off the road from Beverly Hills!

"Listen up, everybody," Coach says. As if he needs to grab our attention. We're all gaping like apes.

"You all know who this is, right?" His face

looks completely satisfied. Like a cat who's swallowed an entire turkey. Man, do we know this guy.

He's here, says Coach, to hang out with us. Watch our moves. Instruct us. To be our *assistant coach*. Jeez! At this news, it's amazing all the Tigers don't swoon to the floor. But we don't. We're too stupefied.

"One thing," Coach adds, "nobody breathes his name, understood? Our new assistant wants to remain anonymous — to keep cameras from snooping around."

Right now nobody can breathe anything. But somehow guys pipe up with "*Yo juro*," "Scout's honor" — even though there are no scouts here — and "I swear on the grave of my hamster."

Then Coach Tree (my name for the wandering all-star) steps forward and says, "*Buenos días.*" That snaps the spell. The Tigers can no longer control themselves. They totally swarm the guy. He hugs everyone and they hug him. And he laughs and laughs.

At home we're discussing this coach thing over supper. *Chiles rellenos,* which Mami and Abuelita prepared together. For this dish you need *poblano* chilies, the black-green glossy kind. Abuelita says you count the veins to pick the hottest ones. Some people prefer bland, but we want those strong enough to blow your head off. Once the skins are roasted and steamed off, you stuff the rest with meat or cheese and dunk them in flour. Then, with stiff coats of egg whites, they fry in oil, floating like hot islands. Last touch, a drizzle of tomato sauce.

To help out, I usually chop the onions, wearing ski goggles that Abuelita and I got at a yard sale. So my tears don't dilute the sauce. One thing I know, if on my own, *por lo menos,* I could always fix *chiles rellenos.*

☆

Our whole family loves basketball. Even Abuelita. Probably even our cat, who sits in

Abue's skimpy lap to watch all games. Especially we love the Lakers. We know the names of all the players, their numbers, their stats. We are wild for their announcers, Chick and Stu, and given the chance, we would vote Chick in for president.

My brother's both excited and skeptical about Coach Tree, the barrio interloper. Luis is three years older than me. Maybe that's why he's untrusting.

"His motive must be money," Luis says, studying his mangled fork, a garbage-disposal victim. But his eyes say no way can that be. The school district's wish list has a focus on *books,* not on NBA coaches.

"Yeah," I say, "like we've got a gushing oil well at school to turn into dollars at will."

Luis burns me a look, so I say, "So cut my heart out and fry it for dinner."

Everyone, including him, laughs at this Aztec humor.

Papi finishes his stuffed chili pepper. *"Ay, qué delicia."* He almost sings about how delicious it is.

Instead, he exclaims, "You are such a good cook, *mi vida*! It's that *mole* runs in your veins."

All happy, Mami laughs and goes a little red. Then she grows serious and says, "I believe this basketball man has all he will ever need. I believe he is doing this coaching for love only."

That sends Luis' eyes spinning in his skull. I can nearly hear his brain grinding: *Love! Man, don't you know? The world goes on* verde — *the green of dollars.* But he says nothing disrespectful. Neither do I. I plan to just dribble my brains loose while this guy's here. To gain every possible tip. Maybe, with buckets of sweat, I'll become *excelente* at this game.

☆

Coach Tree arrives every morning just about before anyone. He slips into the parking lot in some anonymous car and slowly unfolds himself out. Like a giant and rusted pocketknife. I say he's there *before* most everyone. Actually, at first just about the whole school's waiting for a glimpse of him.

He takes that easily. Just strides along, talking to crowding kids and smiling. Like he's found himself a good home. From a distance, where I'm watching, this reception looks like a tall, calm ship riding a choppy sea.

☆

The new basketball program affects everyone. Not just the big kids. From kinder on up, anyone can play. (Our school is so old, kinder to eighth, all grades are there.)

And they do play — if the ball doesn't bog them down. And even if it does. They just keep trying and trying. That's Coach Tree's real aim.

Though everyone gets a shot at basketball, against other schools it's the older kids who suit up. I'm not world-class, but somehow I make the team. For Coach Tree, the Tigers work like crazy. We don't have much height. But speed, we've got *muchísimo*. And we're okay shooters, too.

To say Coach Tree helps us a lot is the understatement of the millennium. No whistles. No yells. No heaving of chairs. From steady practice and from his calm voice, the fundamentals sink in.

Once, between classes, he stops me in the hall. My nerves get tangled as a fistful of paper clips.

"You're working hard, Arturo," he says, quiet as ever. "Doing good."

¡Caray! Like a warm look from a girl (rare for me), I can live on these words forever.

Before long we're actually winning some games. That's partly due to one guy. José. A natural, you could say. He can steam past all defenders. Fake one way, stutter-step, elevate, shoot, and *swish*! All day, all night, if he has to. Like breathing. José, he can flat *play*.

José's a smooth player, but a real troublemaker. His family's a mess, so he bears a chip on his shoulder the size of a sequoia stump. He's been kicked out of school more times than there are numbers. He'd as soon spit on you as talk. Has *pleitos*, fights, for fun. José's a strong reason why we win. Still, for survival, after practice, wherever he is, our team pretty much vacates the area.

☆

There's a sign on my door: NO SE ACEPTAN CHISMES. But, actually, in my room I allow carloads of gossip. *Chismes* bloom at school, too. Soon everyone knows that Coach Tree's losing things. A pen. A handkerchief. A key chain. Once even a tennis shoe! Next thing I hear, the culprit's José. Word is, he's vending Coach Tree-abilia to guys. Jeez! Stealing from Coach Tree's like stealing from God. My opinion? José's the undisputed king of the *menso*-heads.

If it's true, we all expect that this is the last of him. He ought to depart the team fast. But, after all, it must be a story invented for excitement, because José keeps playing. Weird thing, though. *Mucho muy* strange. Sometimes he asks to shoot hoops with us. Sometimes he says hello.

☆

One night Alicia comes over. To do homework. And snack on Mexican cooking. Crunchy *chicharrón,* with lime juice squeezed on. We gouge it into guacamole, while we're sort of studying. "Sort of" because immediately concentration slips away. The air feels as crackly as the pork rinds. Like Alicia's got something to say.

I mark my book with a tomato, the only thing around.

From nowhere she plunges in. "Coach Tree caught José stealing his stuff."

"Yeah?" I say, low-key, to see where this's going.

"Yeah. And he's letting it slide."

"*¡Mentirosa!*" She's gotta be lying. Amazement must fill my face like the look of a stuffed deer.

"Well, not exactly letting it slide," she says. "Coach Tree sees promise in José. He's spending free time with him. Making him practice ball. Making him study. Coach Tree says he won't *let* him toss his life into the Dumpster."

So Coach Tree works with José, one-on-one. I let that sink in. "Think it'll work?" I ask.

"Yeah, I do."

"Why?"

"Because for the first time in forever, José trusts someone."

After Alicia goes, I'm in my room thinking. About Coach Tree and José. Coach doesn't have to do this. He's lost by choice in our nothing barrio, helping a kid with not many chances.

Even though he's a hardcase, I have hope if Alicia does. And she ought to know. José's her brother.

☆

My grandmother takes a decision. "I prepare *chiles rellenos* for this Coach man."

That said, there's no stopping her. I'm ordered to tell him (*tell* the ex-NBA champ!) that the peppers will arrive today after school — along with my whole family. And they do. In a see-through Tupperware tub. (Not my family, the chilies.)

Coach Tree's waiting in the lunch court with a mob of curious kids when Abuelita gets there.

Like a little broom, she sweeps right up and says, "I am happy to meet. You play basket real good. *Chiles muy excelentes.* Eat."

"Yes, ma'am."

He samples a *chile relleno* with Abuelita cheerfully breathing down his neck and prodding, "*¿Excelente? ¿Excelente?*"

Suddenly, Coach Tree's like some cartoon character, steam puffing from his ears, strangling out words in speech balloons: "Agh! Agh!" I say, "Agh!" too, casting an arrowy stare at Abuelita. She's brought the hottest chilies in the universe! Man. My basketball days are over. Probably my life's over.

"CPR!" some kid shouts. What a *menso*-head! There's no CPR for peppers.

Abuelita turns away, totally mortified. I take that back. She's giggling.

We all hold our breath. Then — "*Graa-ci-us, Sonora. Ex-ell-en-tees,*" Coach Tree gasps.

Everyone loses it, *muriendo de la risa.* Then

Coach Tree wipes tears from his face and bows and shakes Abuelita's hand. He shakes hands with everybody in my family. He laughs and laughs. And over the haze of the hot blacktop, carrying the leftover chili peppers, he walks to his car. Slowly, a tall ship of (smoking) calm.

☆

Luis's right. I find out from Alicia, Coach Tree *is* coaching for money. His relative's a teacher here, so he said he'd help out our school — for the salary-shattering price of one dollar.

I know my limits. In pickup games I hold my own, but I'm not NBA-bound. Still, maybe I could do something like Coach Tree. Something for love. Something that's mine. Though right now, I've got zero idea what. To use one of Papi's favorite words, Coach Tree's a person to emulate.

Piano Lessons

Touch magic, and pass it on.

— old saying

I like to read the *L.A. Times*. Anything, from weather to ads for hair replacement. (Not that that's a problem with me, but you never know.) Sometimes you glean (Raúl's word) most from the shorter articles. Two-paragraphers about Bigfoot, or a dinosaur hatchery in what's now Argentina, or a man who collects flat tires. These satisfy some thirst for weirdness in me.

It's the crack of dawn. *La madrugada.* The most beautiful time, when everything begins again.

Papi's mumbling a news clip to himself, then falls into reading aloud. It's about a load of people, some even kids, who've sneaked into the U.S. from Mexico, on foot. So many, they're nearly smothered inside a flimsy and ancient truck. The vehicle picked them up stateside, miraculously evading authorities, only to be *estrellado*, squashed, on Highway 101 by an out-of-control semi. Many dead, though the final count's not in. Sounds like the score of some game.

"*Siempre lo mismo. Los pobres* desperately seeking for betterment, but often finding worse," Papi says. A tear slides through his voice.

This is one of his themes. How the poor but decent come here to get in on the dream. How they're crushed like *cucarachas* in the path of the strong.

Thinking about those people, suddenly my throat goes tight. Thinking about those people, I miss Mexico.

As if by the power of suggestion, my eyes skip to the obituary page. I do that anyhow sometimes. Creepy, I guess, but there are all kinds of interesting people mentioned in there. Like this article today about Leona Scott. A black lady who grew up in the barrio and never moved away.

The *Times* says she was a "piano prodigy." Jazz, especially. Had talent to spare from the start. She could have been a celebrity, like Ellington and those. But she made a promise. A promise to her teacher to pass her talent on.

So Leona Scott taught barrio kids piano, from the time she was pretty little. Those who wanted to learn — and plenty who didn't.

Most clients couldn't pay her with money. Sometimes they gave her enchiladas or sacks of rice —

even pigs. Once, the obit says, a frightened sow got stuck behind Leona Scott's piano and squealed like a crazed singer. She laughed herself weak and named the sow Aretha and kept it for a pet.

From payment in food, she developed a strong sweet tooth for Mexican *dulces,* candies so sugary they can riddle your teeth with holes on sight. She kept bowls of *dulces* on her piano, in case anyone suffered a "low spell," either a pupil or herself. Soon everyone called her Mama Dulce.

"Love each other. Help each other." That's her quote.

Mama Dulce wrote lots of songs. And a jazz opera. But her main thing was teaching — anyone who came along. Even those with criminal tendencies. The magic of music could help most ailments of body or spirit, she claimed. So she passed the music on.

When Mama Dulce got sick and took to bed, word quietly rippled through the barrio. People began arriving at her door. Pupils and ex-pupils and their parents and grandparents. And musicians she'd played with at some time in her life. And musicians she hadn't played with but who just admired her. And people who didn't even know her at all except what their neighbors had told them.

The line of visitors wound around her block like an endless keyboard. Many carried small but struggling livestock. Others, smarter maybe, brought plants and CDs. And, *claro,* Mexican *dulces.*

Then the piano playing began. All day her pupils came and played stuff from "Chopsticks" right on up. One famous jazz pianist played a piece he wrote for her called "Payment in Kind." If she didn't know before, she knew then — her magic passed on.

Mama Dulce had some kind of blood disease. She died at the age of thirty-three.

☆

My browse through the paper's suddenly interrupted.

"¡Rosa! ¡Turo! ¡Luis! *¡Ven!*"

Papi's all in a fluster. *Un pánico total.*

We come on the run. When Papi shows this type of emotion, the problem's gotta be big.

"*¿Qué pasa?*" all three of us ask.

"I need your immediate help! Drop everything, *niños*!" he says with urgency. "*¡Es el día de la amistad!*"

Valentine's Day.

Mami's just left for shopping with Flor Morales, her *comadre*. Now's Papi's chance to launch his top-secret project.

It's no secret from us. Definitely not. Like a fevered bank robber, he's been planning this for months. Going over the steps again and again when Mami's not around: the *pretexto* to get her away for a while; the materials involved; the timing; the accomplices — us.

Our barrio's no place of palaces. Just simple homes from the twenties or so. Some homes in the neighborhood have columns of stone. Or small stone walls around them. Or lines of stone down the sides, like big, bulgy buttons on *mariachi* pants. You can tell Mami loves these houses. She sort of sighs each time she passes one. Papi's plan is this: to paint rows of stones on the front of our house. It would be *carisisísimo* to put real ones.

So the *familia* Rodriguez becomes a painting machine.

Luis and I grab piles of old newspapers squirreled away for this day. Rosa gets the brushes. She loves secret things, so, among rushes of whispers and giggles, she hid them in her dollhouse one time when Papi smuggled them home.

After a changing frenzy, we're wearing baggy old clothes. Like a scarecrow family.

Puffing with urgency, Papi lugs out cans of paint. So everyone can consult it, next to the doorbell, he tacks up his design for the mural of stones. We open the paints. Seagull colors. White and greys. Like the birds that sometimes patrol these skies.

A good smell floats up. Like newness. Like beginnings.

We pick up our brushes.

"*¿Listos?*" Papi asks.

"*¡Listos!*"

We're ready. And we dive in. As scheduled with Flor, we've got two hours to complete this masterwork.

Even Rosa's more in control than Papi — and she's pretty worked up. All frantic, he paces back and forth, taking the role of *maestro de obras,* checking constantly for errors or drips that could mar Mami's porch. The scene's like an old-time painter's workshop — a frenzy of activity and noise — as stones bloom into being. Papi flutters and mutters like a dove on drugs, "*Con cuidado.* With care." "We want no *fracasos.*" "Bigger, I think." "Whiter, I think." "Bolder, I think." "*Sólo una idea.* Just a thought."

"*Calma, Papi, calma,*" I say, trying to tranquilize him.

"You better paint," kids Luis. "Busy hands, sane minds."

I nearly *see* this idea splash in Papi's mind. Like a jumping fish. With sudden emotional fervor, he grabs a brush. In a psycho swing, he goes the other way — from manager to painter.

"*¡Todos callados!* No one speaks!" he commands. "I must have *silencio* to create! Can't you see? I am Siqueiros! I am Orozco! I am Rivera! I am *El Supremo*!"

"You are *El Loquito*!" we shout.

"*¡Claro!*"

Papi rocks with laughter and points his paint-bloated brush at us — carefully.

Above our commotion, Luis' radio roars at top volume. Then there's a pause. The announcer says: "*La próxima canción es* 'Payment in Kind,' *de Bixby Waters. Es un homenaje a la Mamá Dulce, reina de la música, quien falleció el día de hoy.*"

The next song's an homage to Mama Dulce.

I stop painting. I listen to the song and look up into the wide blue sky.

"*¿Quién tiene hambre?*" Abue asks at the height of things. Whether there's hunger here or not, she carries out foods to sustain painters.

That's how we spend the next two hours — being crazed Mexican muralists.

When Mami comes home and sees all those deformed boulders adorning her house — and all those splattered-up painters laughing and now dabbing each other — she nearly faints from happiness. She hugs Papi. She looks at the stones. She hugs us all. She looks at the stones again. She notices that one of these carries a small red heart saying: *te quiero*. She hugs Papi, and she cries.

☆

I lie in bed looking out at the night's *piñata*-spill of stars. The paint smell's strong in our house. I'm trying to sleep in spite of it, thinking about those stones we painted for Mami — and about love. Not the kind that causes you pain and rebuffment, as Raúl calls being thrown away by girls, but love like my parents' kind. Nothing flashy. Just plain and strong, like stones.

I think about people sardined in trucks. Trying to help their families, and far from home.

I think about Mama Dulce, who's dead so young. She could have made headlines. So what? Quietly, she did something else.

What can *I* do? I wish I knew.

In L.A. there's bad. Druggies. Gangs. Thieves, lifting stuff from houses like army ants. Then there's this.

"Love each other. Help each other."

Yeah, I think. And then I sleep.

The River

Nobody sees this warrior
he is so small —
but his struggles are large.
— "Ant," poem

The L.A.'s a swindle of a river. Most years it's nonexistent, its bed of concrete parched as an old scroll. When it does fill up, insane swimmers toss themselves in tire tubes into the furious froth, then drown as easily as moths. Papi says no beast in the air or on the earth can beat the foolishness of the human. He's right.

Today, on my way home from school, I'm walking beside this "river." Alone. I like to come here and forget the rush of L.A. To let my thoughts just fly. Like sprays of birds across the sky. I don't feel lonely a bit. I just sit and think and watch the driftweeds pass, watch the dark trickle of water gleam its way along. Here, what's important stands big. What's not, shrinks. I learn a lot from the silence.

What I most love about this place is the graffiti blooming in the river channel. Letters like colorful balloon animals shriek all the stale sayings: *¡Viva la raza!* Antonio! #1! *¡Número Uno!* Gringo go home! I hate to reveal this to the artist otherwise known as Idiot, but the gringos *are* home.

Really, what I most love about this place is it reminds me of someone. Ms. Cloud. Since when I moved here, she's been at my school. The librarian.

Actually, Ms. Cloud's a past-tense person. Our "careers" moved along side by side, sort of like rickety railroad tracks. When I met her is as clear in my head as the first lick of my first ice-cream cone. Chocolate.

Now I sit down on the concrete riverbank and let the scene scroll back:

It's our first time at the library. Even though I'm kind of old, I'm clutching Mami's hand — and maybe she's clutching mine a little, too. For my whole family, *la biblioteca* is a place of reverence. Where you're courteous. And quiet. And read books that lift you up. The library is a place where you can better your life. And the librarian? Like an angel, wings pressed like white ferns under her sweater. A being close to God. So for us it doesn't hurt her image to have the name of Cloud.

On the door's a quote: "Stock your minds and you can move through the world resplendent." Frank McCourt.

I don't get completely what this means, but I like it. Especially the resplendent part.

Nervously, Mami and I walk the rows. Staring, staring at all the books. Knowing they contain much possibility.

A person floats up to us, quiet as a cloud. She asks, "May I help you find a book?" Her eyes have a look in them that I can only say is full-twinkle. And that's Ms. Cloud's personal way, full-twinkle or zero.

Her question puts a stop to our breathing. But nothing stops Ms. Cloud, not even two tongue-tied strangers. She asks about my interests. I don't know. I don't know anything in this moment.

But Mami becomes brave enough to say, "My son, Arturo, he likes to laugh."

Next thing I know, *Sideways Stories from Wayside School*'s filling my hand.

Man, does Ms. Cloud know kids! Before, I didn't much like to read. Most books were dull as dust. Or breakfast cereal, which our family locks out of the house. We'd rather eat plates of grass. As Abuelita says, "In this *casa,* we do not eat false foods." We eat things with *taste.*

ANYWAY, about this sideways book. It features a sour and fiendish teacher who turns kids into apples on her desk. For me, the English in it's a sweat and a half. But worth it. After this experience, I stick with Ms. Cloud's tips.

I'm a good reader. Plus, even if something's too hard, I'll struggle it out. I'm the ideal victim for this person. Once, a lot later, when my grip on English is good, she reveals to me the books *I, Juan de Pareja* and *The Moves Make the Man.* *¡Híjole!* I'm gone on books.

Although her name's soft-sounding, Ms. Cloud's tough. A warrior in a way. Our library's from pre-dinosaur times. It's got titles like *Old Tales of Japan* (1947), *The Folding Father* (1938), *Two Little Navajos Dip Their Sheep* (1937), *Three Smart Squirrels and Squee* (1942), and so on. Many are falling to pieces, like trees dropping leaves.

Especially the science stuff's ancient. Ms. Cloud can't stand that. So she works on the school district, which is poor. And the PTA, which is poor, and just about doesn't exist. Sometimes she gets us kids, who are poor, to wash cars, to earn money for the library. She even promises to kiss a pig (on the snout) for each donation. She's a bulldog deluxe. Never quits scraping, scritching, scratching everyplace. For books. For us.

One day the library windows are blaring with banners: BOOK BONANZA! READ YOUR BRAINS LOOSE! Soon the library's sardined with curious kids. Turns out "an unknown benefactor" (a secret and big giver) has yanked us into modern times, with encyclopedias, dictionaries, fiction, nonfiction, photography, biography, zoo-ography — you name it. This gift of books is piled dramatically on the library floor, like heaps of apples wind-shaken off trees.

Man, what a scene! *¡Es una locura!* An uproar! A pandemonium! Excited kids, including me, run and squeal and grab books and clutch them close, and smell them, like beautiful flowers, maybe to be sure they're real. And they read, standing up or hunkering or plopped on the floor. One little kid gets so red in the face, he has to go see the nurse — with his book, because he won't let go. Ms. Cloud's beaming — but close to a real tear-burst.

We keep reading when we can — even at recess and lunchtime. Every day, after school, we help Ms. Cloud sort out the books. Our school's so excited, it holds a boisterous *Gracias*-for-the-Books parade. They hope our noise will swell over L.A. so the unknown benefactor will hear our thanks. We're noisy enough. No problem.

☆

In the midst of the book furor, I swallow a shark's eye. Not as part of the frenzy, just on the side. A move of pure *machismo*. I get sucked into it like this:

Rat Nose works at *la marqueta* after school. The butcher shop's his favorite area there because it's full of gross stuff. Chicken feet and livers and gizzards. One day he comes up to me, all hush-hush.

"Look what I got," he says, rifling his pocket and shoving a grey and staring blob right in my face.

"What's *that*?"

"Shark's eye. Dare you to swallow it."

"How much?"

"Fifty cents."

"*¡Ándale!*"

"TURO'S SWALLOWING A SHARK'S EYE!" Rat Nose barely blares the cry, before a cheering section forms. Everyone shoves close to see.

"Ger-OSSSSS!"

"*¡Vas! ¡Vas! ¡Vas!*" Guys chant and egg me on.

For effect, I roll the jelly-like eyeball in my hand like a squishy marble. I rest it on my tongue, then — pop — down it in one gulp.

Cheers ungulf me. *Vatos* engulf me. I'm in my glory. I'm a hero.

Rat Nose pays up.

"How much'd you get?" asks Raúl.

"Fifty cents."

"Fifty cents! *¡Estás chiflado!* I wouldn't swallow a piece of lettuce for fifty cents!"

Okay, so I'm a dumb hero.

"Next time I'll do it for five bucks," I announce.

Next time? I am super-*chiflado*!

☆

Ms. Cloud. Another reason the name suits her is she's a total *misterio*, a mystery. Mostly, kids know a lot about teachers. Where they live. What car they drive. Their personal status. (Married, in *luto*, with *novio*, free.) But with her, in street language, "nobody don't know nothin'." Dressed in her no-style-at-all *ropa* and nun-shoes, she floats in and out of school too early or too late for anyone to gain information.

Overall, this barrio's pretty poor. But maybe she's worse off. Maybe she's embarrassed about her circumstances.

I, for one, can't exist with mystery. After a long time of fevered wondering, I build up a strong need to know. To know about Ms. Cloud. So, one night, when supposedly I'm studying at Raúl's, I follow her. Shadow her after everyone's gone from school. Hefting a bag of books, she walks along. It's a long, dark way. Beside the L.A., falsely named a river, I creep behind her, hanging a safe distance back.

While we walk, a crazy idea spurts into my brain. *What if she's a bag lady, headed for some cardboard house?* My heart squeezes like a fist. What a *menso*-head I am! I really like Ms. Cloud. I'd hate to cause her shame.

Suddenly, she stops, looks quickly around, then

punches one of those long-distance openers to a car, which, to me, give the effect of a terrorist setting off a bomb.

Jeez! What am I saying, "car"? This is a long, low, gleaming, luxury machine. A black Jaguar.

Really, Ms. Cloud doesn't have to punch anything. Because — *¡púfalas!* — like a genie, a guy leaps from the front seat and opens her door.

"Good evening, Ms. Cloud," he says. "Was it a good day?"

Like it's an answer, she says, "I love these girls and boys."

Quickly, she slips into the Jag and plunges off in a costly purr of high octane. I watch, dazed, till the last red of her taillights blinks out. *No hay duda* — she's embarrassed by her circumstances.

The unknown benefactor's unmasked. Like Zorro making a slipup.

I keep this to myself. Her secret's her secret.

But soon more secrets are revealed. One day Ms. Cloud's at school, dealing with overdue books and fines; one day — *¡púfalas!* — she's gone. Our school becomes a gossip factory. The *chisme* is, Ms. Cloud has had no proper credentials all these years! *Es* shocking. To some, this is a Garden-of-Eden-class sin. Full accreditation's required. In their mouths, "required" sounds like a word forged from steel. So Ms. Cloud's fired. *Se acabó la cosa.* That's that.

My family's *horrorizada* beyond belief.

"*¡Qué barbaridad!*" That's Papi's reaction, and as high as he goes on the harsh-language scale. "What a barbarity is this, to release a person from service of great love, and great value. All for a piece of paper. There is such a thing as lenience. There is such a thing as flexibility."

On this night, Mami enters the kitchen and begins to cook — a *mole*, complicated and dangerously spicy.

☆

Many agree with us. Credentials aren't everything. Surely we can make some "arrangement," a word that holds the stretchability of a giant rubber band. Nearly the whole barrio unites on this point. All feel the empty place left when Ms. Cloud departs.

Noisily, we seek her return, carrying blaring signs and picketing. We just throw our hearts out there. Get our emotions totally involved. Even Mega Mango comes forth to make noise on Ms. Cloud's behalf. *Crrrrrink! Crrrrink!* How I rake that gourd for her.

But no arrangement's made. The school board stiffens its back. After all, they've been *engoñados.* Swindled. Tricked. What a *fracaso.* Because of a piece of paper, our librarian's gone. I feel *triste.* Like the sadness of an empty pocket. To get her back, I'd gulp down a hundred shark eyeballs. I'd kiss the noses of pigs.

Once more, Papi proves right: No beast in the air or on the earth can beat the foolishness of the human. Worst part for me is, I don't get to tell her good-bye. I can't say *gracias* for giving me books.

Actually, it's not so bad. She's pretty *lista.* I bet she already knows.

☆

I'm sitting here in graffiti-heaven. The afternoon has stretched itself to grey. Far away, crackles of lightning sizzle the sky. Wind bullies the trees. And it starts raining. Smelling of wet weeds and wet Cyclone fences and wet concrete. Slowly, I get up and start walking home. I stop at the exact spot where our librarian vanished in her Jag, like I'd mentally bookmarked that place.

Maybe someday I could be a book-warrior, like Ms. Cloud. Maybe I'd be good at that. . . .

Just like in third grade, I still like to laugh. To myself I say, *I hope this very* minuto *she's in some other barrio — in full-twinkle — and full disguise — fully resplendent, spouting the glory of books.* At this, I *do* laugh. Out loud. I enjoy my grey solitude all the way home. And the rain comes down.

The Band

When was it that the players recaptured all the notes
still throbbing in the dark and returned them to
the brass throats of their exhausted instruments?
When was it that the band went home?
— "The Morning After, Mexico," poem

*T*onight Mega Mango's got a gig. In the high-school gym. Maybe because he feels deep, rhythmic bonds to us, or because we can't drive yet, Papi drives us — and all our stuff —

to the high school, about ten blocks away. It's a complicated process.

Papi's car is a Studebaker, a model no longer made. He found it, with the aid of God, he says, in a vacant lot. Just resting there waiting for him, he's convinced, year by year falling to ruin. He and Leño Morales, his *compadre*, hauled it home hunk by rusted hunk and restored it to full glory. Papi named it Valentín, for his Western movie hero, Valentín de la Sierra.

Valentín's guacamole green. With a long, snubbed nose. It looks like a monster dragonfly that has no wings. Because of its age, the car has a top speed of forty miles per hour. So it doesn't do freeways. Because of its design, dragonfly slim, its passenger load is small. I don't care. I hope when I get my license I can drive it.

Now, in sizzling September, Papi's navigating our band down the barrio's small backstreets. They give off a good smell of sun-softened tar. We're wedged inside Valentín, crushing our tropical shirts, bright enough to compete with jungle parrots. It's the drummer's idea we dress like this. He's from Veracruz, palm-tree land, same as my friend Raúl.

"'Insane in the membrane. Insane in the *braaaaain*.'" I'm singing, totally jazzed about tonight.

The faithful and law-abiding Valentín hauls us and our bulky instruments in three separate shifts, never exceeding twenty-five miles per hour, the posted speed. Its blunt insect nose bores bravely through the thick smog. Because the car lacks air-conditioning, each load simmers inside like Thanksgiving turkeys. I think, *Guitars could warp in this heat.*

On the last pass — the group I'm in — a car swings from the curb in front of our house. A car full of guys openly swigging Tecate beer from cans. Wearing jackets with macho emblems and bulgy wraparounds that throw off purple tinges.

Like big fly eyes. They wheel alongside Valentín, nearly close enough to scrape paint, taunting Papi about the car's looks and speed. (*Claro,* no cops in sight.)

I know them. The ones who nearly flattened us that day on the way to school. They look like they could give out a real pounding.

"*Oye, pinche viejo,* get a horse! Better yet — get a jackass, old man!"

This type of thing happens in the barrio on a regular basis. Papi always tells us, for confrontations what you want to be is calm. Not say anything in heat. Loose-mouthed guys get busted up — or shot.

To stay silent. *¡Qué coraje!*

Without a flinch, Papi drives on, face rigid. Like the carving of an Aztec god.

Those guys hassle him the whole way, with any name they want to throw out. One pours beer on Valentín. Just a slosh, like he'd rather suck it down than waste it. By the time we regroup at school, our shirts are pasted to our bodies like damp feathers. Not just from the heat.

Now those *menso*-heads squeal away in scorches of tire-rubber, laughing. That scalds my brain. How can they menace my father, this beautiful man?

He's the real macho, I believe, strong enough to be gentle.

"Thanks, Papi," I say quietly. I hope he knows I also mean *be careful*. "Thanks, Señor Rodriguez," say the rest of Mega Mango respectfully, barely above Valentín's buzz. Papi lifts a hand. He'll be back after the dance.

☆

The gym's like an airplane hangar, tall and domed. The floor's of pine planks, once varnished to a gloss, no doubt; now with an overall scuffed finish. The place holds an odor I love. Of wood and stale sweat and chewing gum and more sweat and of the tough rubber skins of all the basketballs ever dribbled here. I breathe deep to take this inside me.

Excitement ripples my veins, from hanging with Luis and his friends. I try to act cool, to hide my age.

We bring in our instruments, all but the piano provided by the school. Everyone makes sure his is still in tune, after the jungular journey inside Valentín. There's lots of twanging and thumping. The guitars especially need reworking of nearly all their pegs. *Claro,* the gourd's unfazed.

The gym looks pretty okay. Stage draped with black curtains for a plain backdrop against our colorfulness. Ceiling looped with crepe paper limp with late summer. In the center, a mirror-ball dangles like an indoor moon. Soon, if things go well, couples will surge to our music, swoon beneath the ball of silver.

☆

Party time. Those punks still crawl at the edge of my brain. But I hum to wedge them out. A few teachers stiffly take up positions. Like trees. On the lookout for trouble-outbreaks. While we warm up, kids start trickling in, all tentative, their voices an overall hum of whispers and giggles.

They arrive in ones and twos, usually of separate sexes. Some are dragging their tall-heeled shoes, as though having second thoughts about how *excelente* an idea it is to attend a school dance. Other couples just plunge in, dressed with zest and laughing, the girls bird-legged, with hairdos of extremes, like dark waterfalls or high wasp nests. The guys with smooth fade haircuts and hoop earrings like pirates. The shoes of these pairs blaze with excessive polish, proclaiming they're ready to *dance*.

And they do. Mega Mango blasts out (or sighs) its full, fervent repertoire, of merengues and cumbias and salsas: *"Terco Corazón," "Cumbia de la Muerte," "Acompáñame Civil."*

Though the audience doesn't know it, for my mother the band plays what she always attempts

to sing at home, *"Ojalá que Llueva Café."*
Mami's addicted to coffee; this song expresses her
hope that one fine day coffee will rain down and
flood the countryside.

Soon everyone's got the fever. Even the football players who've wandered in. Wide, invincible
hulks. They dance like they're still at football practice, like they're swimming in refried beans —
but, hey, at least they dance. The whole place's
thrashing with motion. Couples pressed close.
Like fresh and warm tortillas. The gym smells like
melting hair spray and aftershave.

Our band has no actual musical plan. We go with
the feel of things, with dancers' moods. Above
everything, the mirror-ball spins, sending swarms
of light over the walls like stirred-around stars.

In this *muy* cool moment, the dancing suddenly stops. Ceases. We quit playing and look for
the problem, though I *feel* what it is. That gang
from Creepland that taunted Papi enters in full
swagger, bringing the general feel of threat. Even

from this distance, I can see the leader's hands bunching, as if itching for *pleito.*

These guys are easy to evaluate. Measly types. Typical lizard-brained *vagos,* equipped for only fighting. For them the world's a sour place where everything that happens twists to a personal insult. The least lift of an eyebrow; an offensive color; the intake of the wrong amount of breath.

"Having *mucho* fun?" The head lizard flames his demon grin, his words bleared by beer.

The invaders have high hair, like rooster combs. They aren't dressed for dancing, wearing pants so baggy, one false breath and they could slip off. Too baggy to tell if they're harboring weapons.

Fear spears my *tripas.* Then a weird wave of heat sprawls over me, and I'm sweating *galones,* soaking my shirt. Mami'll never scrub the armpit smell out.

The next thing, ugly words, like toads, spurt from many mouths. The chaperone-teachers lamely try some enforcing, but scuffling and shoving break out, anyway. So much for weapons. If armed, the punks'd be slashing or firing by now.

Some dancers, including the linemen, pick up on this and form a barrier of bulk between the punks and the rest of us. Then comes the big staredown. Like at the OK Corral. These guys reveal they're just display. Too measly to hold a gaze long. Our guys advance; the reptile boys back up. Too easily.

They don't want a fight — now. They just enjoy sending fear-ripples over people.

Inspired by this show of righteous force, Mega Mango recovers its spunk. The drummer scrolls out a drumroll as they move back and back. The guitar players strum and sing the song *"Vaya con Dios,"* though that's not what they really mean. Just when the gang reaches the door, Luis taunts them with a few choppy notes, well known as standing for the worst thing you can say of someone's mother.

Ya estuvo. Lizard's got a temper on him. He

smolders at my brother, "*Oye,* trumpet-boy, I know where you live."

☆

The dance is dead. When Papi meets us, from everyone at once, he hears hot bursts about the standoff. Lips so stiff, his words about to crack, Papi says, "This is a thing that greatly angers me. A thing for worry."

Grimly, warily, he shuttles Mega Mango home. I'd like to walk. To feel the ground beneath my feet. But that's too dangerous. Anyplace, those junior punks could be lying in the weeds. . . .

I ask myself, *What's the good of starting up a band? Starting anything? Lowlifes just come and turn it ugly.*

The Lunch Box

Grown-up to girl: "When you're big,
what will you be?"
Girl to grown-up: "A police! A police!"
— overheard at the market

*T*hose punks from this weekend's dance totally take over my mind, even though I try to shove them out. Once wronged, these *tipos* rivet on re-venging. They could jump Luis anytime.

Maybe it's not such a hot idea, but I'm attempting *The Count of Monte Cristo,* the all-time payback book. If she knew, Ms. Cloud would be in full-twinkle over this choice. It's a major reading struggle for me, but worth every sweat bead. Man, this Edmond Dantès character's expert at dealing out *venganza.*

Lizards invade my dreams.

"Don't be scared," comes a voice.

"I'm not scared."

"Don't be scared."

"I'm not — *I am.*"

Someone hugs me. Like an angel. Like Mami. I crumple and cry.

☆

Rosa's six. She's named after Mami. But Papi, whose eyes gleam up like that Taco Bell dog's eyes every time she enters his range of vision, calls her "Rosie-Posie-Dominosie." It's a long story:

My father works in a Mexican furniture store.

His job's no flashy big-time *trabajo.* He's a sales-
man. Not too high up or too low down. Just
hanging in the middle. In his three years there,
he's never missed a day of work. Mami says Papi's
like good earth under that store. He's there and
there and there. The owner gave him a zipper-
jacket, once, in commemoration of loyalty. It's
kind of cheesy. A sheeny gold fabric, the color of
a sicko pumpkin. He doesn't say so, but I know
Papi's excessively proud of it, the way he cares for
that jacket.

At lunchtime every day my father and his
furniture-selling pals play dominoes. The Mexican
kind. At a restaurant called La Adelita. They like
it there because the owners and employees are all
of one family. Real friendly. They love dominoes,
too, so they allow Papi's group to linger after
lunch.

They let them spread out in the back room and
smack their tiles around — *¡Cuas! ¡Cuas!* — till

they get jumpy about getting back to work. Actually, they don't get *that* jumpy. Papi's boss's a domino freak. A real *fanático*. Since he usually plays, too, there's no problem. At this time, jokes fly over the table, like flocks of migrating birds. Jokes especially about the double-four, called *la suegra*, the mother-in-law. It's the one you want to get rid of — ha-ha!

Mami says with a twinkle, "How that store continues going, it's the guess of anyone."

ANYWAY, Rosa *adores* Papi. The smallest thing he does, like touching his nose with his tongue, will impress her forever. In every way, she wants to emulate him, he says, enjoying the roll of that word over his teeth. She emulates him by "playing dominoes." Her own kind. Scrunched on her belly on the rug at night. Making snaking links of tiles. So, she's Rosie-Posie-Dominosie.

Rosa means "rose" in Spanish, but also it means "pink." So my sister thinks everything she owns should be of that color and no other. She refuses to wear anything but dresses, as pink and fluffy as big, wide birthday cakes.

Tomorrow, Rosa's starting first grade. So, of course, she *needs* a pink lunch box. A pink lunch box is the one thing that will complete her life. Who buys one for her? Papi. It's got a baby dinosaur on it, with big glazy Disney eyes, highly lashed like clumps of black grass. Cute enough to make you puke. Rosa won't be apart from this hideous rectangle of bubble-gum pink.

Today Rosa gets a letter from her "pen pal," Leo Love, the guy who rescued our cat. Last week Mami helped her write him:

Dear Mr. Leo Love,
   How are you? I am fine. My cat is fine. How are you?

                              Love,
                              Rosa Rodriguez

Leo Love writes back:

Dear Rosa,
  I am very well, thank you. I am not sneezing, but I miss your little cat. Perhaps she could visit me. Perhaps you could bring her — and some corn fungus. I am tempted to experience that dish.
                    Sincerely, your friend,
                    Leo Love

Everyone sees the letter and feels warmth again toward this man.

"I must organize *huitlacoche* for *El Estimado*," says Abuelita in a surge of cooking plans. Rosa's so happy, she refolds the letter on its exact creases and puts it safely in her lunch box.

☆

Tonight will forever be tattooed in the skin of my mind.

We're in the kitchen, snacking on delicious

tacos de chilorio, a product of pork so high in fat, on the grease from one can you could slide across the barrio. From last year, our Day of the Dead altar's still up on one counter. With fake marigold flowers and sugar skulls and an image of the *Virgencita* and two small flags, American and Mexican, and a postcard of *The Last Supper,* which Abuelita calls *The Last Dinner,* and a photograph of my grandfather, smiling and young.

"So, Rosie-Posie-Dominosie, where will your lunch box sleep?" Papi asks when it's her bedtime. Like it's alive.

Puke-o-rama!

Rosa says, "With me."

"Mi amor," Mami wheedles, "let's let it sleep here, in the kitchen."

Rosa's mouth starts to tremble. Her eyes shine with oncoming tears.

"Mami's right. It will be happy here," Papi says. "Next to the pink milk pitcher."

That line of reasoning, featuring the color

pink, convinces Rosa. So she allows herself to be pried from her beloved lunch box — separated, just for the night. Papi sets it on the windowsill above the sink.

As he does this, I see him give a quick glance outside. He does this every night. Is he expecting something — like I am?

Like a family of large moths, we're hovering under the kitchen bulb, saying "Good night. *Buenas noches.* Good night." Rosa says *"buenas noches"* to her lunch box. That's when disaster erupts.

Just before it happens, I hear the dark purr of a car. A beast creeping on stealthy tires. Then I hear gunfire. The slap of bullets into the flesh of our house. The room's raining plaster and glass and choking dust. No one knows how we get there, but we're smack on the floor — ¡*Cuas!* ¡*Cuas!* — like living dominoes.

Next thing, along with a window, Rosa's lunch box explodes to smithereens. Outside, you can bet, Mami's Valentine "stones" are totally strafed.

In a shriek of rubber, the car plunges down the street. It seems like half an hour before anyone can breathe, let alone mouth a word. All I can think of is Leo Love's shredded letter and lunchbox shards. Like the remains of a pink asteroid smashed into Mars. That lunch box could have been one of us. One of us could be dead.

All's quiet. Except for the heartbeat-ticking of the kitchen clock.

"*¿Todos bien?* Everyone's okay?" At last Papi gasps and checks us all for wounds. Again and again, he checks, trembling. God is mediating; we're dazed and scraped with glass, but no one's injured badly. Though he seems calm, I can tell Papi's enraged. His jaw's clamped like a padlock. And Mami — her eyes hold a hurt so deep, you couldn't dig it out with a backhoe.

Abuelita's real quiet. For about the first time in her whole, long life.

And Rosa, she's totally frozen.

"*Mi reinita,* my little queen." Papi hugs Rosa.

"*¡Qué barbaridad!*" he whispers. To shoot at people — in their homes *además* — is an utter barbarity. He tries to speak, words stumbling like a broken-winged bat, to explain this terrible thing. Nothing he says can do that.

I feel totally rasped out. Like a gourd.

I feel my life melting to something else. Something sickening, like a picture at our library of watches melting. Zombielike, I wonder, *Will our kitchen ever recover from this?* What I really mean is, will *we?*

Two minutes ago there was Rosa, happiness itself, in her fuzzy pink robe. Twisting like cotton candy on a stick. I wish I could have kept her from this lesson in ugliness. Now, not all the pink things in this world would make her smile. It just breaks me down. I have no words. Stiff with fear, Rosa's not six anymore.

I know where you live. The words burn my brain. Those *malditos* who did this. Coming here, hunting Luis — and he's at a friend's, not even home. They're kicked-around dogs, going on *maldad*. So mean, they'd blast roses right out of some lady's flower garden, just to hear their guns.

Well, they got their revenge on us, so they won't be back. That's how it works. I wish I could hurt them — real bad. But I can't. They're gone.

We form a ring, a ring of Rodriguezes. Like a kind of prayer. No one says so, but I think we all know, right here we're holding all that matters in the whole world. We're holding each other.

☆

We're still like that when the police come. A man and a woman arrive at the door, with badges, bright gleams of authority.

The police. In the barrio, the people are often victims. The conditions of their lives make them angry and untrusting. In this moment, when they arrive, man, that's exactly what *I* am. Angry and untrusting.

Maybe Mami's with *desconfianza* also, thinking of her brush with them. But this is different. This isn't about possums.

The man sizes things up, eyes grey as guns. "I'm Officer Paster," he says.

Rhymes with disaster, I think. Which is what this night is. The cops, mainly the man, ask a lot of questions. Like the kind on TV. But we all know nothing much will be done. Drive-bys happen all the time. Mostly the perps get away.

Still, these two cops don't seem to be used to this. Like us, they seem to feel the horror. They keep low-key and formal, bringing a stiff kind of gentleness into the house.

Rosa hasn't said a word. She hasn't cried. The whole time they're interviewing us, she just stares at her lunch-box remains, which Mami hasn't swept up. The kitchen's such a mess, where does she start?

Officer Paster tries to comfort Rosa. "I'm sorry about your lunch box," he says, figuring it's hers.

When he touches her head, she flinches. Like she won't trust anyone again.

On their way out, to all of us, he says, "I am so sorry." And he means it.

☆

Next day, as the sun lifts, he's here. Officer Paster. At first, I don't know who he is, though. He's wearing grungy Nikes and sweats. Maybe he's been running, trying to sweat out last night's outrage.

For the first time, Papi's missed work. He checks through the curtains, grunts, then opens the door. Mami looks on, silently, Rosa clinging to her. Afraid to let go. Today she's not going to school.

The cop just stands there. Looking like maybe he's butting in.

What's to say? For a minute, it's real quiet.

"It's not much," Officer Paster says finally, "but maybe you'll like it."

Then, awkward and tender, he holds something out to my sister. A rectangle of pink. With *menso*-Disney artwork. A gift lodged forever in the deep-down part of my heart — a hideous and glorious lunch box.

No, it's not much. But this small kindness changes the world. Rosa's eyes go big as plates. She smiles a limp little smile. Then she hugs the lunch box — and she cries.

Inside myself, I say, *Bless you, Officer Disaster.*

Like Papi said when we got our cat back, "When no eyes are upon him, that is a person's true test."

No bigwig's watching Officer Paster. Doesn't matter. I am.

Good things happen in L.A. — just not enough.

☆

In spite of this one event — in spite of Leo Love and Coach Tree and Mama Dulce and Ms. Cloud and Luis and his band and all my family —

I know nobody's really safe. Here, what you love's always at risk.

"What a place is this barrio." I nearly spit the words across the room.

"*Mijo.*" With *cariño*, Papi touches my shoulders and looks into my face. The world seems to wait while he arranges his thoughts. Then slowly he says, "In life there is *bueno* and there is *malo*. If you do not find enough of the good, you must yourself create it." A big speech for him. And I can tell he's not done. After a moment he says, "Remember this thing — any small goodness is of value."

Any small goodness. Pointless to argue. But in my head I snarl, *Yeah, right.*

The Green Needle Gang

Gang: A bunch of armed lowlifes hanging out with intent.
— L.A. resident's definition

In class today I'm a *fantasma*, a ghost. There, but not really. I'm floating somewhere else, brooding. About good and bad. The point of things. Since the shooting, I still feel a fury so hot it scorches my heart. So hard, it scares me.

Tonight I call my friends. No question. They come. Luis's already there. About those wild-reptile gangs stalking the streets — I know now what *I'm* gonna do. Ain't no band, ain't no basketball team. I'm going for *venganza,* man, my kind of revenge. And if I'm lucky, no eyes will be on me.

When we're together, I announce my plan: "*Oigan,* everybody. Listen up," I say. "We're forming our own gang."

☆

"Jeez, Turo, I thought they'd *never* leave!"

That's what Luis says when Mami and Papi finally go off to another *posada.* Abuelita and Rosa go, too. Every year at these Christmas *fiestas,* my parents eat themselves into stupors and stay out late. I imagine them sometimes, lingering with the *compadres,* chatting less and less brightly because of the hour. Like fireflies losing their sparkle.

When they're gone, it's great for me and *Los*

Verdes, the Green Needle Gang, the one I formed. Gives us time for some *fiestas* of our own.

Families stick together, so Luis's one of us. I'm in his band, so he's in my gang.

December's the sucker month. Raúl fell on that name after reading some poem in English class about a wasted land. And, *man,* are we seeking suckers!

Soon as my family turns the corner, the gang slips like cats from the bushes. Dressed dark as *huitlacoche,* in sweaters, gloves, bulky stuff.

It's freezing cold. Wind gulps its way through the garden. While I yank on a black turtleneck and a black knit cap, the rest hiss stuff like "Move it, man!" and *"¡Órale, Turo! ¡Muévete!"*

I dress so fast, I'm all in black, except my jeans (my blue skin, Mami calls them), when Carlos, called "Flan," wheels up the driveway.

He's our getaway guy. Luis' best friend, and the only one of us who can drive legally. Behind the wheel of Maybelline, his mascara-colored pickup, a long Snoopy-style scarf boldly furling from his neck, Flan's something to behold. And, man, can he thread the backstreets of L.A.

Maybelline's motor guns with a sound as thick as Abuelita's *pozole* while we crawl in, hauling stuff for the hit. The hit. Even though we grab ahold of money any way we can, seems we've never got enough for our needs.

All month we prowl the barrio, by truck or by Nike, stalking victims. Got a crop of houses spotted, sure as if we'd painted big red X's on the doors. Like Passover, Rat Nose says. Only we don't pass over the X-ed ones. What we pick out, we nail.

This is no little-kid stuff. It requires planning. And secrecy — to the eleventeenth degree. The stakes are high for us. So we practice like crazy. Like shooting hoops. Till each hit works *muy* fine. A perfect *swish*.

Now our swish-machine's in motion.

"Raúl. Jaime. Rat Nose. Alicia. Luis." I spit their names, sharp, like tacks, making sure everyone's here. They are. Every single time. Every single member of the Green Needle Gang.

I thump Maybelline's cab once.

We lurch off. Sometimes Flan's not too *excelente* with the clutch.

✩

We're all hunched down in the truck bed, watching the Christmas lights and the witch-haired palm trees blur by. Rat Nose's popping his knuckles, making a sound like snapping carrots. A sound that makes me shiver. He always does this before a hit, to pop out his nerves.

I think of my parents at their party. Mami probably assisting her *comadre* with complicated foods; Papi seated at a wobble-legged table with his cronies, happily clicking dominoes, like small, cold bones. If they only knew what we're up to. In Raúl's lingo, they'd expire.

"What's on your busy roach brain?" Alicia asks. Like she can read my mind.

"Just thinking. My folks could see me now, they'd loco-out."

"What kind of word's *that*?" asks Luis, a touch of brotherly acid in his voice.

"A *bueno* one."

"My *jefes* would be proud of our modus operandi," Raúl, Word Man, announces. He says it all inflated. Like he knows Latin or something.

I think, *Two words ain't Latin.*

We're combing a mangy street. Olivo. Under the glaring hubcap moon. Little licks of light lift from some of the houses; others are dead dark.

Quiet as a cat stalking some ratty bird, we're creeping up on our target. Nobody knows her name. Never do. But in this neighborhood, *seguro* it's Señora something-or-other.

Rat Nose's the one who sniffed her out. Just poking his pointy face around. He reported an old lady, lumpy and brown as a potato, lived there, in a dinky, dumpy house. *Todo catiado.* All size of kids scootin' all over, like the ones that lived in that Mother Goose shoe. While they ran around, the old lady fussed over them. While they slept, she plumped down on a groady old sofa on the porch. An old pigeon in a nest of dust, Rat Nose said.

We know their every move, thanks to him. Tonight, when we make our move on them, we hope they'll really loco-out.

Olivo number 73. Flan sidles Maybelline to the curb down the street and cuts her motor in mid-cough.

"Easy pickings." Alicia grins. "Real piece of *pastel.*"

Raúl says, "Go for the jungular vein." Another lame-o tropical joke. Winters especially, his head's wedged in Veracruz.

"Ready or not, Pigeon Woman, here we come." Rat Nose bares his rodent teeth.

My heart bangs so hard, it could pump right

through my chest. What if we get caught? But risk's part of what's so cool. A pumping heart — and getting away with something.

No talk allowed now. Not one word. So I signal with my hand. *¡Vamos!* Go!

Flan, the lookout, hangs back.

The rest of us slink through the shadows. Cats who know the night. We nimble over a hedge and duck behind some thornbushes. I get raked. But I don't care. I feel excessively high.

Ready to rush the house.

Then Raúl trips on his own submarine-size feet. What a major *menso*-head!

"*¡Híjole!*"

"*Cállate la* bleedin' *boca,*" I hiss.

Too late for quiet. A flashlight snaps on. I suck air like it's my last gulp.

"Come out o' there," growls a voice. Deep and dark. Like night.

Jeez! A cop. And he ain't saying ho-ho-ho. Spread out though we are, his eyes quickly take us in, easy as a loose-eyed halibut. I want to bolt, but my Nikes are pure lead.

"What're you kids up to?" Suspicion oozes from every word — every loud word about to give us up.

I can hardly breathe. Finally, my brain kicks in. I mouth, "We're the Green Needle Gang."

That's enough.

"Well, what're you waiting for?" rasps the cop, suddenly dropping to whisper-mode. *"Move!"*

"Hey, thanks, man — er — sir," Rat Nose mumbles with stammering courtesy.

We swish from the bushes in a stiff whisper of green needles. In one swoop, one *diablo* of a rustle, we've got all our stuff on the porch. Another swoop, everyone's piled into Maybelline. Everyone but me. I'm glad it's my turn to hang back. Pigeon Woman deserves this. I punch the bell with quick jabs and leave our signature note: The Green Needle Gang Strikes Again!

Three spurts of the doorbell and I'm airborne.

I plop on top of everyone, now a panting pile. We're scrunched down real low in the truck's belly, Jonah-like, watching the house with binocs the whole time. While Maybelline begins to crawl away, I wait for the biggest rush.

A light snaps on. Like a smear of sickly yellow Kraft cheese. Pigeon Woman pokes her head out, checking the porch, her face drooping like a collapsed balloon. She gonna faint? Nope. She just claps a hand to her mouth and gasps.

"*¡Niños! ¡Niños!* Babies! *¡Ven!*" she shrieks at operatic volume.

And do those babies come! Plumpeting in frenzied loco-motion. Like puppies tumbling over each other. When they see the tree and the food and the toys, I think they'll expire from laughing — and crying. I think I'll expire, from joy.

This is no scruffy, pathetic shrimp we've left. (Jaime's always the final selector. His motto: I can't respect a tree that's shorter than I am.) It's no sequoia, either. Still, it's a plant of some stature. A full-blown *ÁRBOL*, man. Decked to the gills and swamped with gifts, right up to its spiky green knees. One thing about us — we never skimp.

Suddenly, comes a celestial silence, when Pigeon Woman lifts a finger to her lips. She must say something to them, because the whole family shouts in a yappy chorus, "God bless the Green Needle Gang!"

One little kid peers over the porch, Christmas stars in his eyes. "*¡Besitos! ¡Besitos!* I kiss you!" he calls. And he flares out kisses everywhere.

"I kiss you," I whisper into the tender Christmas air.

I feel high as heaven. I feel wide as the ocean. I feel totally resplendent.

☆

Inside the truck bed, we hug each other, octopus-style. Still, we try to hold onto our cool. But I catch the gleam of many tears, shining like ink in the dark.

A cop walks up to the house just then. In a dry voice he sandpapers out, "Trouble, ma'am?"

"*Ay, sí,* officer." The lady's in control now, voice sweet as a psalm. "Kind of trouble we *totalmente* need."

Then I thump the cab. Flan revs Maybelline to life. With a wild clutch-crunching, we barrel away in a rubberized roar.

Raúl, the mad linguist, yells, *"Excelsior!"*

☆

It's pretty quiet on the way home. Too quiet. So finally I say, "Well, we got our wish. They sure did loco-out."

And we do, too — totally — when we get home.

Christmas Presents

Silent night! Holy night!
All is calm, all is bright.

— Josef Mohr

It's Christmastime, and our house is in flames. In every room *nochebuenas,* flowers of Christmas, flare their total joy. The whole place is glopped up with deformed reindeer that Luis and I once made and a *nacimiento* with only two wise men left (a thing that causes Mami to mourn) and Rosa's paper chains.

At this season, I guess we could go up to our eyeballs in owing money, to give stuff to each other. Papi says most people at Christmas make those Visa guys grin from one plastic ear to the other. But we don't go that route. Our family follows the Rodriguez Policy of *Navidad,* of one person giving a present to only one other person.

Careful as picking fleas off lions, we each pull a name from Mami's cookie jar. Everyone's in there. Even Huitla. (One person pulls two names to cover her.) Mami fills the jar with cookies, too, so you can pick your victim and get a cookie simultaneously. Then each one bustles off to hide the secret name in a secret, *secret* place.

It's tough to keep that name hidden. But the toughest part is, for the present, you have to give a part of your heart. Like something you make or write or do. Whatever, that's really from you.

I love this time when everyone's creeping around and slinking his eyes back to make sure no one's watching. It's a time so secret, even the house seems to be whispering.

When the actual opening of presents happens, it's usually as obvious as a fire truck in snow who gave what to whom. But we all play totally *bobo*, like we're perplexed out of our minds.

"Christmas is a time of giving." That's an old saying people have. For us it's also a total time of eating — *mucho* more than usual. Abuelita and Mami cook constantly. And we all nibble and taste things constantly, then waddle around like turkeys being fattened for the kill. Huitla knows something special's going on. She rubs against the refrigerator and purrs like ten cats in one, to coax it to pour out something delicious for her.

☆

One of my favorite things at *Navidad* is our family "tamale-a-thon." To prepare for this, the grown-ups swoop to the market in Valentín, then putt home, with the poor car nearly bursting open its doors with food. Because I'm *el jefe de las cebollas,* the onion boss, all ski-goggled up, I chop-chop-chop excessively now. All worthy dishes carry many onions.

After various potions have burbled on the stove to complete deliciosity, the whole next day — and night if we need more time — we're up to our armpits in stuffings for tamales. We do the pork kind. And chicken. And plainer ones, from fresh corn. Even dessert ones. To remind us how perfectly *locos* we are, these are blushing pink, for Rosa. When we're done, the kitchen's nothing but tamales and tamales and tamales.

Then comes the doling out, even more fun than the mess of creation. This year we give tamales to lots of people. Our friends of the *alma,* the soul, of course. Like the *compadres.* And all members of the Green Needle Gang, although only Luis and I know this part of their lives. Actually, we deliver these bundles in person — in the true Green Needle style.

We add to the tamale list *El Estimado* Leo Love and Officer Paster and his partner and Coach Tree. "*Porque* he loves Mexican cookings extremely," explains Abuelita. Even my name-changer teacher, Miss Pringle, gets tamales. Everyone's teachers get some — except one. I try to track down Ms. Cloud to include her. But she's completely poofed herself from existence. From ours, at least.

☆

It's *Nochebuena,* the night before Christmas. We're gathered by our tree, opening presents. That's our custom, gifts on Christmas Eve. A seventy-eight record from long ago's spinning, and Elvis, Abuelita's favorite — after my grandfather — is groaning to just her, "— on a snowy Christmas night."

The top of the tree has an angel that Rosa made "by herself." That means mostly with Mami's help. It's of white paper with skinny pine-needle wings.

Its teeny-weeny paper halo's the size of a Life Saver candy. No matter how careful we are, it tears off every year. Every year it gets taped back on.

"An angel with no halo! Someone might mistake it for Mami!" Papi throws up his hands all fake-aghast. Then like a deep-down drum, he laughs.

Papi's in charge of rubber-banding the angel to the top of the tree. He handles it like a brittle butterfly. It's pretty ugly, but it's our most beloved ornament.

The presents wait. Shining under the tree. We wait. Expectantly. And a shining Something happens — *Navidad*.

After each present's revealed, after the *ay*'s and sighs, comes the cry, "*Atole* break! *Atole* break!" Then we stop, clink mugs, and sip a gluggy drink as old as the gods themselves.

Already the presents have been magnificent. As Mami says, "To touch the very heart." She herself has received a *mago*, another wise man, squeezed tenderly from clay and painted in the flamboyant style of certain Mexican artists. Clutching it to her chest, she looks at Abuelita with tears in her eyes. To try to throw us off. *¡Ay!* As if she could! We know it's from *El Supremo*, enhancer of porches, painter of stones.

Abuelita gets a choir of angels made by my fumbler-hands from leftover tamale husks. There are five people-angels, one for each of us. And one cat-angel, which looks like a lopsided weasel. To hear her, this present places Abuelita right up there in heaven with happiness.

Even though it's not her turn, Huitla now rips into a catnip bird, made from my old pajamas. A poem goes with it:

> *Huitla, you stay home.*
> *I will pat your fur.*
> *Don't go away.*
> *I love you.*

Rosa's struggled-out words.

At the same time, Luis unwraps a box, blooming with a highly tropical and hand-stitched shirt. He hugs Mami a long time — even though, *claro*, he doesn't know she made it.

When Papi opens his present, he studies it immensely, gaping his mouth like a gasping guppy. It's a thin, limp chain of yarn. Pink. About three miles long. And full of kinks.

"*¡Ay, qué bufanda rosa tan hermosa!*"

He whoops and swoops it around his neck, exclaiming about this beautiful pink scarf.

"*¡Qué bonita! ¡Qué linda! ¡Qué estupenda! ¡Qué adorable, maravillosa y totalmente gloriosa!*"

He goes totally *alocado* and begins plunging around, bellowing an ocean of emotion. Like Vicente Fernandez, the *ranchera* king. Bellowing odes to this gift, the wisp of kinked-up "scarf" flowing behind him like a stretched-out cloud. Huitla finds the *bufanda* pretty *gloriosa,* too. She deserts her bird and darts after it, pouncing and missing, pouncing and missing.

By now the rest of us are twisted in spasms of laughter, except for Rosa, who's singing and dancing, too.

In an exuberance fit, Luis bounces up from the sofa and announces, "For your pleasure, a new song, *'La Bufanda Rosa y Gloriosa.'*" He snags his trumpet and blows forth wild and un-*navideño* sounds.

When the crazies collapse, there's sudden quiet. Like angels entering. In the stillness, Papi says, *"Te quiero,* Rosie-Posie."

"I love you, also, Papi, but —"

"¿Pero, qué?"

"You're not sus-sposed to know it's from me!"

"Then I *don't* know," says Papi.

☆

Elvis's crooning "Silent Night" by the time things come around to me. Because I'm last — and because this night has to last a whole year — I unwrap my present extra carefully.

Es un arbolito. A perfect little wooden Christmas

tree. Worked out in complete detail, from a string of lights and tiny ornaments and a star on top, down to a grinning kid on a bike. The thing that makes me go totally teary — on the tree itself, someone's lovingly painted, like green eyelashes, positively every single green pine needle.

The giver could be one person only.

"Hang it up," Luis says. I hear something rough but soft in his voice.

The tree has a little leather loop. Slowly, I get up. I choose the best branch for it and place it on our tree.

I look around at the faces I love. *Mi familia.* Rodriguezes, warm and sweet and silly, glowing in the candlelight. I feel Christmas well up in me.

Music fills the room. "Silent night! Holy night!"

With my family here, with good people out there in the barrio, it is — totally holy.

☆

A Selected Glossary

☆

Abuelita: Granny
Además: Besides
Ahora: Now
Ahoritita: Right now
Alocado: Crazed
¡Ándale!: Let's go!
Árbol: Tree
Atole: Corn-based drink
¡Ay . . . mi pequeño cactus!: Oh . . . my little cactus!
¡Ay, qué bufanda rosa tan hermosa!: My, what a beautiful pink scarf!
Besitos: Little kisses
Borrados: Erased
Bueno: Good
Buenos días: Good morning
Buey: Ox
Cállate la boca: Shut up
Calma: Calm down
¡Caray!: For Pete's sake!
Cariño: Tenderness; love
Carisisísimo: Super-expensive
Casa: House
Chicharrón: Pork rind
Chilaquiles: Dish made with old tortillas
Chiles rellenos: Stuffed chilies

Chismes: Gossip
Cholos: Lowlifes
Chorizo: Spicy sausage
Claro: Of course
Comadre: Godmother
Compadre: Godfather
¡Cuas!: Slapping sound
Cucaracha: Cockroach
Datos: Information
Desconfianza: Mistrust
Diablos: Devils
Dios mediante: God willing
Diosito: God (affectionate)
¿Dónde está?: Where is she?
Dulces: Sweets
El Loquito: The Crazy One
El Supremo: The Supreme One
Es el día de la amistad: It's Valentine's Day
Es un arbolito. It's a little tree
Es un homenaje a la Mamá Dulce, reina de la música, quien falleció el día de hoy: It's an homage to Mama Dulce, queen of music, who died today
¡Es una locura!: It's a frenzy!
¡Estás chiflado!: You're nuts!

Estimado: Esteemed
Familia: Family
Fanático: Fanatic
Fracasos: Disasters
Galones: Gallons
Gatita: Little cat
Gracias: Thank you
Hijos: Jeez
¡Híjole!: Jeez!
Horrorizada: Horrified
Huitlacoche: Corn fungus
Jefes: Parents
La biblioteca: The library
La madrugada: Dawn
La marqueta: The market
La próxima canción es:
  The next song is
Limones: Limes
Lista: Smart; with it
¿Listos?: Ready
Locos: Crazy
Los pobres: The poor
Luto: Mourning
Maestro de obas: Foreman
Maldad: Evil
Malditos: Bad dudes
Malo: Bad
'Mano: Bro
Mariachi: Traditional
  Mexican musician
Menso: Dumb
¡Mentirosa!: Liar!
Menudo: Tripe soup

Mi amor: My love; my dear
Mi vida: My life; my dear
Mijo: My son
Molcajete: Grinding stone
Mole: Complex chili sauce
Muchachos muy lindos:
  Very nice kids
Muchísimo: A lot
Mucho muy: Very
Muele: Grind
¡Muévete, buey!:
  Move it, moron!
Muriendo de la risa:
  Dying of laughter
Muy: Very
Nacimiento: Crèche
Nahual: Birth animal
Navidad: Christmas
Niños: Children
No hay duda:
  There's no doubt
No se aceptan chismes:
  No gossip allowed
No sé: I don't know
Novio: Boyfriend
Oigan: Listen
Órale: Hurry up
Orgullo: Pride
Oye, pinche viejo:
  Hey, you old jerk
Pastel: Cake
Pavor: Dread
¿Pero, qué?: But what?

Pleitos: Fights
Por las cochinas dudas:
   Just in case
Por lo menos: At least
Por please!: Gimme a break;
   pretty please
Porque: Because
Posada: Christmas party
Pozole: Hearty meat soup
¡Púfalas!: Poof!
*¡Qué adorable, maravillosa
y totalmente gloriosa!:*
   How adorable, marvelous,
   and totally glorious!
¡Qué barbaridad!:
   What an outrage!
¡Qué bonita!: How pretty!
¡Qué coraje!: What anger!
Qué delicia: How delicious
¡Qué estupenda!:
   How stupendous!
¡Qué linda!: How lovely!
¿Qué pasa?:
   What's happening?
¿Quién tiene hambre?:
   Who's hungry?
Ranchera: Traditional music
Rebozo: Shawl
Ropa: Clothing
Salud: Blessing (for sneezes)
Sarape: Blanket
Se acabó la cosa: It's over
Seguro: For sure

Sí: Yes
Siempre lo mismo:
   Always the same
Taquería: Taco stand
Te quiero: I love you
Tipos: Guys
Tlacuaches: Possums
Todo catiado:
   Totally ramshackle
¿Todos bien?:
   Everybody all right?
¡Todos callados!
   Everybody quiet!
Trabajo: Work
Tripas: Gut
Triste: Sad
Un idiota de primera:
   A first-class idiot
Un pánico total:
   A complete panic
Vagos: Vagrants
¡Vas!: Go!
Vatos: Guys; dudes
Vaya con Dios:
   Go with God
Ven: Come
Venganza: Revenge
Virgencita: Virgin of
Guadalupe (affectionate)
¡Viva la raza!: Long live
   the Mexican people!
Ya estuvo: That's it
Yo juro: I swear